MARTHA and SKITS

Susan Meddaugh

HOUGHTON MIFFLIN COMPANY BOSTON

Walter Lorraine Books

For Linda and John

www.houghtonmifflinbooks.com

Library of Congress Cataloging-in-Publication Data

Meddaugh, Susan.
  Martha and Skits / Susan Meddaugh
  p. cm.
  Summary: Martha watches as the new dog her family brings home goes through all the troublesome phases of being a puppy, and even though he does not develop Martha's ability to speak, Skits displays his own unique talent.
  RNF ISBN-13: 978-0-618-05776-4
  PA ISBN-13: 978-0-618-60917-8
  [1. Dogs—Fiction.] I. Title.
  Pz7.M51273 Mak 2000
  [E]—dc21   00-023988

Printed in Singapore
TWP   10 9 8 7 6
4500442607

Martha's family had a little surprise for her.

Within days of Skits's arrival, the house was in chaos.

Martha enjoyed the show from the safety of her chair.
She remembered being a puppy.

But one day Skits did
something unforgivable.

Martha decided it was time to take charge.
"There are only two rules around here," she told Skits.

She explained how the letters in the soup went up to her brain instead of down to her stomach.

"Someday you'll be old
enough for your own
bowl of alphabet soup,"
Martha told him.
But Skits wasn't listening.

At first Skits was an equal opportunity chaser and chewer,
but he soon began to specialize. *Anything airborne*. He
couldn't resist a flying object. Outside . . .

uh
oh.

or inside

"GRRRRow up," said Martha.

Before long, Skits did.

But nothing really changed.
Skits continued to chase anything flying
through the air.
He just couldn't help it.

One morning Skits found his family gathered in the kitchen.
"It's time," they announced.
Instead of one bowl of alphabet soup and one bowl of kibble,
there were two bowls of alphabet soup on the kitchen floor.

Everyone watched as Skits ate his bowl of soup. They leaned closer, eager to hear his first words.

"That's it!" they said. "More soup."
The family made sure that every letter in the alphabet was
there in the bowl. Again they waited as Skits finished his
second helping of alphabet soup.

This time he said:

ARF!

Martha wondered about Skits's brain. Was it too small? Maybe there wasn't room for twenty-six letters.

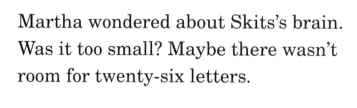

"Oh well," Father said. "I guess two talking dogs was too much to expect."

Skits wandered out to the yard and lay down. He knew his family was disappointed in him. Martha was special. He was not.

His gloomy thoughts didn't last for long.

ARF!

Skits always enjoyed a good bug chase.
But this was his first taste of yellow jacket.

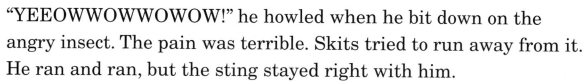

"YEEOWWOWWOWOW!" he howled when he bit down on the
angry insect. The pain was terrible. Skits tried to run away from it.
He ran and ran, but the sting stayed right with him.

Many miles later Skits came to a stream and gulped down the cold water. At last his mouth felt better.
Then he looked around and realized something. He was lost.

When Skits didn't come home, the whole family set out to look for him. They walked down every street and talked to everyone they met, but they didn't find Skits.

That night, while her family made signs, Martha stayed by the phone. "I'm sure he's okay," she thought. "Maybe someone has found him."

On the other side of town, Skits spent the longest, loneliest night of his life.
"If only I could talk," he thought.

The next morning the family gathered their signs
and began the search all over again.
Everything reminded them of Skits.

"Skits would love this,"
said Helen sadly, pointing
to a sign on the tree.

"That's where he'll be!" shouted Martha. "All those flying objects in
one place all afternoon!"
"You're right!" said Helen. "*He can't help it.*"

Martha and her family watched and waited through every event at the Frisbee competition. Multicolored disks sailed through the air for hours, yet there was no sign of Skits.

The final contest of the day was the Chase for the Golden Frisbee.
As the yellow disk sailed across a blue sky, every dog in the park,
including Martha, took off after it.

Then from the opposite end of the park came a flash of familiar fur.

It was a dog so fast and focused on the flying disk that all the other dogs stopped in their tracks. All the other dogs except Martha.

A cheer went up from the crowd.
"What a catch!" they shouted. "That dog wins the Golden Frisbee!"
On the way home Helen said, "Martha. You missed the Frisbee.
You never missed before."
Martha just smiled.

That night Martha and Skits each ate a bowl of alphabet soup.
Skits opened his mouth, then closed it. He still couldn't speak.
"That's OK," Martha told him. "You are a specialist in flying objects."